Flora McQuack

By Penny Dolan

Illustrated by Kay Widdowson

Special thanks to our advisers for their expertise:

Adria F. Klein, Ph.D.
Professor Emeritus, California Sto
San Bernardino, Califor

Susan Kesselring, M./
Literacy Educator
Rosemount-Apple Valley-Eagan (Minne

PICTURE WINDOW BOOKS
Minneapolis, Minnesota

Levels for *Read-it!* Readers

- Familiar topics
- Frequently used words
- Repeating patterns

- New ideas
- Larger vocabulary
- Variety of language structures

- Challenges in ideas
- Expanded vocabulary
- Wide variety of sentences

- More complex ideas
- Extended vocabulary range
- Expanded language structures

A Note to Parents and Caregivers:

Read-it! Readers are for children who are just starting on the amazing road to reading. These beautiful books support both the acquisition of reading skills and the love of books.

The RED LEVEL presents familiar topics using common words and repeating sentence patterns.

The BLUE LEVEL presents new ideas using a larger vocabulary and varied sentence structure.

The YELLOW LEVEL presents more challenging ideas, a broad vocabulary, and wide variety in sentence structure.

The GREEN LEVEL presents more complex ideas, an extended vocabulary range, and expanded language structures.

When sharing a book with your child, read in short stretches, pausing often to talk about the pictures. Have your child turn the pages and point to the pictures and familiar words. And be sure to reread favorite stories or parts of stories.

There is no right or wrong way to share books with children. Find time to read with your child, and pass on the legacy of literacy.

Adria F. Klein, Ph.D.
Professor Emeritus
California State University
San Bernardino, California

First American edition published in 2005 by
Picture Window Books
5115 Excelsior Boulevard
Suite 232
Minneapolis, MN 55416
877-845-8392
www.picturewindowbooks.com

First published in Great Britain by Franklin Watts, 96 Leonard Street,
London, EC2A 4XD

Printed in the United States of America.

Library of Congress Cataloging-in-Publication Data
Dolan, Penny.
Flora McQuack / by Penny Dolan ; illustrated by Kay Widdowson.
p. cm. — (Read-it! readers)
Summary: Although the other ducks scoff, Flora McQuack patiently sits on an egg that
she has found, waiting for it to hatch.
ISBN 1-4048-0561-3 (hardcover)
[1. Ducks—Fiction. 2. Eggs—Fiction.] I. Widdowson, Kay ill. II. Title. III. Series.
PZ7.D6978Fl 2004
[E]—dc22   2004007618

Flora McQuack bustled along the water's edge. There, in the tall grass beside the lake, sat the McPeck sisters.

"Hello, ladies!" Flora cried.
"Ssssss … ," they hissed. "Get away
from our nests. Everyone knows
you're a bad-luck duck!"

"Meanies! I wouldn't hurt a tadpole," Flora hissed back.

Flora moved away, but she had tears in her eyes. She thought of the McPeck sisters and the smooth eggs in their nests.

Flora sighed. Never, in her whole life, had she laid an egg.

Flora waddled off around the lake, all alone.

Suddenly, she noticed something smooth and oval among the stones on the bank.

"Goodness me!" she exclaimed.
"It's a poor orphaned egg."
Flora nestled warmly against it.

"Ha, ha! You silly duck," laughed the McPeck sisters as they swam past. "That will never hatch."

"Oh, mind your own business,"
quacked Flora. "It's my egg now,
and I'm going to hatch it, no
matter how long it takes."

It took a very long time. Spring turned to summer, and all the other eggs had hatched.

No sound came from Flora's egg,
but still she sat on it patiently.

At last, Flora heard something.
First there was a tapping, then a
creaking and a cracking, and finally
the shell broke open.

The strange creature opened its surprised eyes. It had four short legs, a long tail, and no feathers. It did not look like a duck at all!

"Mama!" cried the little creature,
stumbling toward Flora.

"Oh!" exclaimed Flora. "You are a strange little thing, but I love you!"

Flora marched to the edge of the lake. "Come along now," she said to her new baby. "Time for a swimming lesson."

Splash! Flora plunged into the water, and the little creature followed her.

When Flora looked behind her, her new baby had disappeared beneath the ripples.

"Oh no! I've drowned the little thing!" she gasped.

But up popped the little creature, lake weeds dripping from its mouth. Gurgling happily, it dived again. Flora gazed at the trail of sparkling bubbles.

The McPeck sisters would never
be able to make fun of such a
good swimmer.

Up it popped again, splashing
Flora joyfully.

"Mind your manners," she scolded gently. "Don't behave like a little monster!"

And away swam Flora and her strange, long-necked baby across the wide waters of Loch Ness.

Levels for *Read-it!* Readers

Read-it! Readers help children practice early reading
skills with brightly illustrated stories.

Red Level: Familiar topics with frequently used words and
repeating patterns.
I Am in Charge of Me by Dana Meachen Rau
Let's Share by Dana Meachen Rau

Blue Level: New ideas with a larger vocabulary and a variety
of language structures.
At the Beach by Patricia M. Stockland
The Playground Snake by Brian Moses

Yellow Level: Challenging ideas with an expanded vocabulary
and a wide variety of sentences.
Flynn Flies High by Hilary Robinson
Marvin, the Blue Pig by Karen Wallace
Moo! by Penny Dolan
Pippin's Big Jump by Hilary Robinson
The Queen's Dragon by Anne Cassidy
Sounds Like Fun by Dana Meachen Rau
Tired of Waiting by Dana Meachen Rau
Whose Birthday Is It? by Sherryl Clark

Green Level: More complex ideas with an extended vocabulary
range and expanded language structures.
Clever Cat by Karen Wallace
Flora McQuack by Penny Dolan
Izzie's Idea by Jillian Powell
Naughty Nancy by Anne Cassidy
The Princess and the Frog by Margaret Nash
The Roly-Poly Rice Ball by Penny Dolan
Run! by Sue Ferraby
Sausages! by Anne Adeney
Stickers, Shells, and Snow Globes by Dana Meachen Rau
The Truth About Hansel and Gretel by Karina Law
Willie the Whale by Joy Oades

A complete list of *Read-it!* Readers is available on our Web site:
www.picturewindowbooks.com